Making the House a Home

Edgar A. Guest

Contents

MAKING THE HOUSE A HOME

BY

Edgar A. Guest

Here's our story, page by page,
Happy youth and middle-age,
Smile and tear-drop, weal and woe
Such as all who live must know--
Here it is all written down,
Not for glory or renown,
But the hope when we are gone
Those who bravely follow on
Meeting care and pain and grief
Will not falter in belief.

Making the House a Home

We have been building a home for the last fifteen years, but it begins to look now as though it will not be finished for many years to come. This is not because the contractors are slow, or the materials scarce, or because we keep changing our minds. Rather it is because it takes years to build a home, whereas a house can be builded in a few months.

Mother and I started this home-building job on June 28th, 1906. I was twenty-five years of age; and she-- well, it is sufficient for the purposes of this record to say that she was a few years younger. I was just closing my career as police reporter for the Detroit "Free Press," when we were married. Up to a few months before our wedding, my hours had been from three o'clock, in the afternoon, until three o'clock in the morning, every day of the week except Friday. Those are not fit hours for a married man--especially a young married man. So it was fortunate for me that my managing editor thought I might have possibilities as a special writer, and relieved me from night duty.

It was then we began to plan the home we should build. It was to be a hall of contentment and the abiding place of joy and beauty. And it was all going to be done on the splendid salary of twenty-eight dollars a week. That sum doesn't sound like much now, but to us, in January, 1906, it was independence. The foundation of our first home was something less than five hundred dollars, out of which was also to come the extravagance of a two-weeks' honeymoon trip.

Fortunately for all of us, life does not break its sad news in advance. Dreams are free, and in their flights of fancy young folks may be as extravagant as they wish. There may be breakers ahead, and trials, days of discouragement and despair, but life tells us nothing of them to spoil our dreaming.

We knew the sort of home we wanted, but we were

willing to begin humbly. This was not because we were averse to starting at the top. Both Mother and I had then, and have now, a fondness for the best things of life. We should have liked a grand piano, and a self-making ice box, and a servant, and an automobile right off! But less than five hundred dollars capital and twenty-eight dollars a week salary do not provide those things.

What we could have would be a comfortable flat, and some nice furniture. We'd pay cash for all we could, and buy the remainder of the necessary things on time. We had found a wonderful, brand-new flat which we could rent for twenty-five dollars a month. It had hard-wood floors, steam heat, two big bedrooms, a fine living room with a gas grate, a hot-water heater for the bath, and everything modern and convenient. To-day the landlord would ask ninety dollars a month for that place and tell you he was losing money at that.

With the rent paid, we should have eighty-seven dollars a month left to live on. The grocery bill, at that time, would not run more than twenty dollars a month; telephone, gas, and electric light would not exceed ten dollars a month; the milkman and the paper boy would take but little, and in winter time a ton of coal per month would be sufficient. Oh, we should have plenty of money, and could easily afford to pledge twenty dollars a month to pay for necessary furniture.

It will be noticed that into our dreaming came no physician, no dentist, no expenses bobbing up from unexpected sources. Not a single bill collector called at the front door of our dream castle to ask for money which we did not have.

If older and wiser heads suggested the possibility of danger, we produced our plans on paper, and asked them from whence could trouble come? To-day we understand the depth of the kindly smile which our protests always evoked. They were letting the dreamers dream.

At last the furniture was bought on the installment plan and the new flat was being put in order. It called for a few more pieces of furniture than we had figured on, and the debt, in consequence, was greater; but that meant merely a few months more to make payments.

It was fine furniture, too! Of course it has long since ceased to serve us; but never in this world shall that dining set be duplicated! For perfection of finish and loveliness of design, that first oak dining table will linger in our memories for life. The one we now have cost more than all the money we spent for all the furniture with which we began housekeeping; and yet, figuring according to the joy it has brought to us, it is poor in comparison.

And so it was, too, with the mahogany settee, upholstered in green plush, and the beveled glass dresser, and the living-room chairs. We used to make evening trips over to that flat merely for the joy of admiring these things--our things; the first we had ever possessed.

Then came the night of June 27th. We had both looked forward to that wonderful honeymoon trip up the lakes to Mackinac Island, and tomorrow we were to start. But right then I am sure that both Mother and I wished we might call it off. It seemed so foolish to go away from such a beautiful flat and such lovely furniture.

The honeymoon trip lasted two weeks; and one day, at Mackinac Island, I found Mother in tears.

"What the matter?" I asked.

"I want to go home!" she said. "I know I am silly and

foolish, but I want to get back to our own house and our own furniture, and arrange our wedding presents, and hang the curtains, and put that set of Haviland china in the cabinet!"

So back we came to begin our home-building in earnest.

The rent and the furniture installments came due regularly, just as we had expected. So did the gas and electric light and telephone bills. But, somehow or other, our dream figures and the actual realities did not balance. There never was a month when there was as much left of our eighty-seven dollars as we had figured there should have been.

For one thing, I was taken ill. That brought the doctor into the house; and since then we have always had him to reckon with and to settle with. Then there was an insurance policy to keep up. In our dream days, the possibility of my dying sometime had never entered our heads; but now it was an awful reality. And that quarterly premium developed a distressing habit of falling due at the most inopportune times. Just when we thought we should have at least twenty dollars for ourselves, in would come the little yellow slip informing us that the thirty days' grace expired on the fifth.

But the home-of-our-own was still in our dreams. We were happy, but we were going to be still happier. If ever we could get rid of those furniture installments we could start saving for the kind of home we wanted.

Then, one evening, Mother whispered the happiest message a wife ever tells a husband. We were no longer to live merely for ourselves; there was to be another soon, who should bind us closer together and fill our lives with gladness.

But--and many a night we sat for hours and planned and talked and wondered--how were we to meet the expense? There was nothing in the savings bank, and much was needed there. Mother had cherished for years her ideas for her baby's outfit. They would cost money; and I would be no miserly father, either! My child should have the best of everything, somehow. It was up to me to get it, somehow, to.... If only that furniture were paid for!

Then a curious event occurred. I owed little bills amounting to about twenty-one dollars. This sum included the gas, electric light, and telephone bills, on which an added sum was charged if unpaid before the tenth of the month. I had no money to meet them. I was worried and discouraged. To borrow that sum would have been easy, but to pay it back would have been difficult.

That very morning, into the office came the press agent of a local theatre, accompanied by Mr. Henry Dixey, the well-known actor. Mr. Dixey wanted two lyrics for songs. He had the ideas which he wished expressed in rhyme, and wondered whether or not I would attempt them. I promised him that I would, and on the spot he handed me twenty-five dollars in cash to bind the bargain. If those songs proved successful I should have more.

The way out had been provided! From Mr. Dixey's point of view, those songs were not a success; but from mine they were, for they bridged me over a chasm I had thought I could not leap. I never heard from that pair of songs afterward; but neither Mother nor I will ever forget the day they were written.

It meant more than the mere paying of bills, too. It

taught us to have faith--faith in ourselves and faith in the future. There is always a way out of the difficulties. Even though we cannot see or guess what that way is to be, it will be provided. Since then we have gone together through many dark days and cruel hurts and bitter disappointments, but always to come out stronger for the test.

The next few months were devoted to preparations for the baby, and our financial reckonings had to be readjusted. I had to find ways of making a little more money. I was not after much money, but I must have more. All I had to sell was what I could write. Where was a quick market for a poor newspaper man's wares?

My experience with Mr. Dixey turned me to the vaudeville stage. I could write playlets, I thought. So while Mother was busy sewing at nights I devoted myself to writing. And at last the first sketch was finished. At the Temple Theatre that week was the popular character actor, William H. Thompson. To him I showed the manuscript of the sketch, which was called "The Matchmaker." Mr. Thompson took it on Tuesday; and on Friday he sent word that he wished to see me. Into his dressing-room I went, almost afraid to face him.

"It's a bully little sketch," said he, as I sat on his trunk, "and I'd like to buy it from you. I can't pay as much as I should like; but if you care to let me have it I'll give you two hundred and fifty dollars--one hundred and fifty dollars now, and the remaining hundred next week."

I tried to appear indifferent, but the heart of me was almost bursting with excitement. It meant that the furniture bill was as good as paid! And there would be money in the bank for the first time since we were married! The deal was made, and I left the theatre with the largest sum of money I had ever made all at once. Later someone said to me that I was foolish to sell that sketch outright for so little money.

"Foolish!" said I. "That two hundred and fifty dollars looked bigger to me than the promise of a thousand some day in the future!"

Once more the way out had been provided.

And then came the baby--a glorious little girl--and the home had begun to be worth-while. There was a new charm to the walls and halls. The oak table and the green plush settee took on a new glory.

I was the usual proud father, with added variations of my own. One of my pet illusions was that none, save Mother and me, was to be trusted to hold our little one. When others would take her, I stood guard to catch her if in some careless moment they should let her fall.

As she grew older, my collars became finger-marked where her little hands had touched them. We had pictures on our walls, of course, and trinkets on the mantelpiece, and a large glass mirror which had been one of our wedding gifts. These things had become commonplace to us--until the baby began to notice them! Night after night, I would take her in my arms and show her the sheep in one of the pictures, and talk to her about them, and she would coo delightedly. The trinkets on the mantelpiece became dearer to us because she loved to handle them. The home was being sanctified by her presence. We had come into a new realm of happiness.

But a home cannot be builded always on happiness. We were to learn that through bitter experience. We had seen white crepe on other doors, without ever thinking that some day it might flutter on our own. We had witnessed sorrow, but had never suffered it. Our home had welcomed many a gay and smiling visitor; but there was a grim and sinister one to come, against whom no door can be barred.

After thirteen months of perfect happiness, its planning and dreaming, the baby was taken from us.

The blow fell without warning. I left home that morning, with Mother and the baby waving their usual farewells to me from the window. Early that afternoon, contrary to my usual custom, I decided to go home in advance of my regular time. I had no reason for doing this, aside from a strange unwillingness to continue at work. I recalled later that I cleaned up my desk and put away a number of things, as though I were going away for some time. I never before had done that, and nothing had occurred which might make me think I should not be back at my desk as usual.

When I reached home the baby was suffering from a slight fever, and Mother already had called the doctor in. He diagnosed it as only a slight disturbance. During dinner, I thought baby's breathing was not as regular as it should be, and I summoned the doctor immediately. Her condition grew rapidly worse, and a second physician was called; but it was not in human skill to save her. At eleven o'clock that night she was taken from us.

It is needless to dwell here upon the agony of that first dark time through which we passed. That such a blow could leave loveliness in its path, and add a touch of beauty to our dwelling place, seemed unbelievable at the time. Yet to-day our first baby still lives with us, as wonderful as she was in those glad thirteen months. She has not grown older, as have we, but smiles that same sweet baby smile of hers upon us as of old. We can talk of her now bravely and proudly; and we have come to understand that it was a privilege to have had her, even for those brief thirteen months.

To have joys in common is the dream of man and wife. We had supposed that love was based on mutual happiness. And Mother and I had been happy together; we had been walking arm in arm under blue skies, and we knew how much we meant to each other. But just how much we needed each other neither of us really knew--until we had to share a common sorrow.

To be partners in a sacred memory is a divine bond.

To be partners in a little mound, in one of God's silent gardens, is the closest relationship which man and woman can know on this earth. Our lives had been happy before; now they had been made beautiful.

So it was with the home. It began to mean more to us, as we began each to mean more to the other. The bedroom in which our baby fell asleep seemed glorified. Of course there were the lonely days and weeks and months when everything we touched or saw brought back the memory of her. I came home many an evening to find on Mother's face the mark of tears; and I knew she had been living over by herself the sorrow of it all.

I learned how much braver the woman has to be than the man. I could go into town, where there was the contagion of good cheer; and where my work absorbed my thoughts and helped to shut out grief. But not so with Mother! She must live day by day and hour by hour amid the scenes of her anguish. No matter where she turned, something reminded her of the joy we had known and lost. Even the striking clock called back to her mind the hour when something should have been done for the baby.

"I must *have another little girl," she sobbed night after night. "I* must have another little girl!"

And once more the way out was provided. We heard of a little girl who was to be put out for adoption; she was of good but unfortunate parents. We proposed to adopt her.

I have heard many arguments against adopting children, but I have never heard a good one. Even the infant doomed to die could enrich, if only for a few weeks, the lives of a childless couple, and they would be happier for the rest of their days in the knowledge that they had tried to do something worthy in this world and had made comfortable the brief life of a little one.

"What if the child should turn out wrong?" I hear often from the lips of men and women.

"What of that?" I reply. "You can at least be happy in the thought that you have tried to do something for another."

To childless couples everywhere I would say with all the force I can employ, adopt a baby! If you would make glorious the home you are building; if you would fill its rooms with laughter and contentment; if you would make your house more than a place in which to eat and sleep; if you would fill it with happy memories and come yourselves into a closer and more perfect union, adopt a baby! Then, in a year or two, adopt another. He who spends money on a little child is investing it to real purpose; and the dividends it pays in pride and happiness and contentment are beyond computation.

Marjorie came to us when she was three years old. She bubbled over with mirth and laughter and soothed the ache in our hearts. She filled the little niches and comers of our lives with her sweetness, and became not only ours in name, but ours also in love and its actualities.

There were those who suggested that we were too young to adopt a child. They told us that the other children would undoubtedly be sent to us as time went on. I have neither the space here nor the inclination to list the imaginary difficulties outlined to us as the possibilities of adoption.

But Mother and I talked it all over one evening. And we decided that we needed Marjorie, and Marjorie needed us. As to the financial side of the question, I smiled.

"I never heard of anyone going to the poorhouse, or into bankruptcy," I said, "because of the money spent on a child. I fancy I can pay the bills."

That settled it. The next evening when I came home, down the stairway leading to our flat came the cry, "Hello, Daddy!" from one of the sweetest little faces I have ever seen. And from that day, until God needed her more and called her home, that "Hello, Daddy" greeted me and made every care worth while.

The little home had begun to grow in beauty once more. That first shopping tour for Marjorie stands out as an epoch in our lives. I am not of the right sex to describe it. Marjorie came to us with only such clothing as a poor mother could provide. She must be outfitted anew from head to toe, and she was. The next evening, when she greeted me, she was the proud possessor of more lovely things than she had ever known before. But, beautiful as the little face appeared to me then, more beautiful was the look in Mother's face. There had come into her eyes a look of happiness which had been absent for many months. I learned then, and I state it now as a positive fact, that a woman's greatest happiness comes from dressing a little girl. Mothers may like pretty clothes for themselves; but to put pretty things on a little girl is an infinitely greater pleasure. More than once Mother went down-town for something for herself--only to return without it, but with something for Marjorie!

We pledged to ourselves at the very beginning that we would make Marjorie ours; not only to ourselves but to others. Our friends were asked never to refer in her presence to the fact that she was adopted. As far as we were concerned it was dismissed from our minds. She was three years old when she was born to us, and from then on we were her father and her mother. To many who knew her and loved her, this article will be the first intimation they ever have received that Marjorie was not our own flesh and blood. It was her pride and boast that she was like her mother, but had her father's eyes. Both her mother and I have smiled hundreds of times, as people meeting her for the first time would say, "Anyone would know she belonged to you. She looks exactly like you!"

Marjorie made a difference in our way of living. A

second-story flat, comfortable though it was, was not a good place to bring up a little girl. More than ever, we needed a home of our own. But to need and to provide are two different propositions. We needed a back yard; but back yards are expensive; and though newspapermen may make good husbands they seldom make "good money."

One evening Mother announced to me that she had seen the house we ought to have. It had just been completed, had everything in it her heart had wished for, and could be bought for forty-two hundred dollars. The price was just forty-two hundred dollars more than I had!

All I did have was the wish to own a home of my own. But four years of our married life had gone, and I was no nearer the first payment on a house than when we began as man and wife. However, I investigated and found that I could get this particular house by paying five hundred dollars down and agreeing to pay thirty-five a month on the balance. I could swing thirty-five a month, but the five hundred was a high barrier.

Then I made my first wise business move. I went to

Julius Haass, president of the Wayne County and Home Savings Bank, who always had been my friend, and explained to him my difficulties. He loaned me that five hundred dollars for the first payment--I to pay it back twenty-five dollars monthly--and the house was ours.

We had become land owners overnight. My income had increased, of course; but so had my liabilities. The first few years of that new house taxed our ingenuity more than once. We spent now and then, not money which we had, but money which we were going to get; but it was buying happiness. If ever a couple have found real happiness in this world we found it under the roof of that Leicester Court home.

There nearly all that has brought joy and peace and contentment into our lives was born to us. It was from there I began to progress; it was there my publishers found me; and it was there little Bud was born to us. We are out of it now. We left it for a big reason; but we drive by it often just to see it; for it is still ours in the precious memory of the years we spent within its walls.

Still, in the beginning, it was just a house! It had no

associations and no history. It had been built to sell. The people who paid for its construction saw in its growing walls and rooftree only the few hundred dollars they hoped to gain. It was left to us to change that house *into a* home. It sounds preachy, I know, to say that all buildings depend for their real beauty upon the spirit of the people who inhabit them. But it is true.

As the weeks and months slipped by, the new house began to soften and mellow under Mother's gentle touches. The living-room assumed an air of comfort; my books now had a real corner of their own; the guest-chamber--or, rather, the little spare-room--already had entertained its transient tenants; and as our friends came and went the walls caught something from them all, to remind us of their presence.

I took to gardening. The grounds were small, but they were large enough to teach me the joy of an intimate friendship with growing things. To-day, in my somewhat larger garden, I have more than one hundred and fifty rosebushes, and twenty or thirty peony clumps, and I know their names and their habits. The garden has become a part of the home. It is not yet the garden I dream of, nor even the garden which I think it will be next year; but it is the place where play divides the ground with beauty. What Bud doesn't require for a baseball diamond the roses possess.

Early one morning in July, Bud came to us. Immediately, the character of that front bedroom was changed. It was no longer just "our bedroom;" it was "the room where Bud was born." Of all the rooms in all the houses of all the world, there is none so gloriously treasured in the memories of man and woman as those wherein their children have come to birth.

I have had many fine things happen to me: Friends have borne me high on kindly shoulders; out of the depths of their generous hearts they have given me honors which I have not deserved; I have more than once come home proud in the possession of some new joy, or of some task accomplished; but I have never known, and never shall know, a thrill of happiness to equal that which followed good old Doctor Gordon's brief announcement: "It's a Boy!"

"It's a Boy!" All that day and the next I fairly shouted it to friends and strangers. To Marjorie's sweetness, and to the radiant loveliness of the little baby which was ours for so brief a time, had been added the strength and roguishness of a boy.

The next five years saw the walls of our home change in character. Finger marks and hammer marks began to appear. When Bud had reached the stage where he could walk, calamity began to follow in his trail. Once he tugged at a table cover and the open bottle of ink fell upon the rug. There was a great splotch of ink forever to be visible to all who entered that living-room! Yet even that black stain became in time a part of us. We grew even to boast of it. We pointed it out to new acquaintances as the place where Bud spilled the ink. It was an evidence of his health and his natural tendencies. It proved to all the world that in Bud we had a real boy; an honest-to-goodness boy who could spill ink-- and would, if you didn't keep a close watch on him.

Then came the toy period of our development. The once tidy house became a place where angels would have feared to tread in the dark. Building blocks and trains of cars and fire engines and a rocking horse were everywhere, to trip the feet of the unwary. Mother scolded about it, at times; and I fear I myself have muttered harsh things when, late at night, I have entered the house only to stumble against the tin sides of an express wagon.

But I have come to see that toys in a house are its real adornments. There is no pleasanter sight within the front door of any man's castle than the strewn and disordered evidences that children there abide. The house seems unfurnished without them.

This chaos still exists in our house to-day. Mother says I encourage it. Perhaps I do. I know that I dread the coming day when the home shall become neat and orderly and silent and precise. What is more, I live in horror of the day when I shall have to sit down to a meal and not send a certain little fellow away from the table to wash his hands. That has become a part of the ceremonial of my life. When the evening comes that he will appear for dinner, clean and immaculate, his shirt buttoned properly and his hair nicely brushed, perhaps Mother will be proud of him; but as for me, there will be a lump in my throat--for I shall know that he has grown up.

Financially, we were progressing. We had a little more "to do with," as Mother expressed it; but sorrow and grief and anxiety were not through with us.

We were not to be one hundred per cent happy. No one ever is. Marjorie was stricken with typhoid fever, and for fourteen weeks we fought that battle; saw her sink almost into the very arms of death; and watched her pale and wasted body day by day, until at last the fever broke and she was spared to us.

Another bedroom assumed a new meaning to us both. We knew it as it was in the dark hours of night; we saw the morning sun break through its windows. It was the first room I visited in the morning and the last I went to every night. Coming home, I never stopped in hall or living-room, but hurried straight to her. All there was in that home then was Marjorie's room! We lived our lives within it. And gradually, her strength returned and we were happy again.

But only for a brief time.... Early the following summer I was called home by Doctor Johnson. When I reached there, he met me at the front door, smiling as though to reassure me.

"You and Bud are going to get out," said he. "Marjorie has scarlet fever."

Bud had already been sent to his aunt Florence's. I was to gather what clothing I should need for six weeks, and depart.

If I had been fond of that home before, I grew fonder of it as the days went by. I think I never knew how much I valued it until I was shut out from it. I could see Mother and Marjorie through the window, but I was not to enter. And I grew hungry for a sight of the walls with their finger marks, and of the ink spot on the rug. We had been six years in the building of that home. Somehow, a part of us had been woven into every nook and corner of it.

But Marjorie was not thriving. Her cheeks were pale and slightly flushed. The removal of tonsils didn't help. Followed a visit to my dentist. Perhaps a tooth was spreading poison through her system. He looked at her, and after a few minutes took me alone into his private office.

"I'm sorry, Eddie," he said. "I am afraid it isn't teeth. You have a long, hard fight to make--if it is what I think it is."

Tuberculosis had entered our home. It had come by way of typhoid and scarlet fevers. The specialist confirmed Doctor Oakman's suspicions, and our battle began. The little home could serve us no longer. It was not the place for such a fight for life as we were to make. Marjorie must have a wide-open sleeping porch; and the house lacked that, nor could one be built upon it.

And so we found our present home. It was for sale at a price I thought then I should never be able to pay. We could have it by making a down payment of seventy-five hundred dollars, the balance to be covered by a mortgage. But I neither had that much, nor owned securities for even a small fraction of it.

But I did have a friend: a rich, but generous friend! I told him what I wanted; and he seemed more grieved at my burden than concerned with my request. He talked only of Marjorie and her chances; he put his arm about my shoulders, and I knew he was with me.

"What do you need?" he asked.

"Seventy-five hundred dollars in cash."

He smiled.

"Have a lawyer examine the abstract to the property, and if it is all right come back to me."

In two days I was back. The title to the house was clear. He smiled again, and handed me his check for the amount, with not a scratch of the paper between us.

I suggested something of that sort to him.

"The important thing is to get the house," he said. "When that is done and you have the deed to it and the papers all fixed up, you come back and we'll fix up our little matter." And that is how it was done.

So into our present home we moved. We had a bigger and a better and a costlier dwelling place. We were climbing upward. But we were also beginning once more with just a house. Just a house--but founded on a mighty purpose! It was to become home to us, even more dearly loved than the one we were leaving.

For four years it has grown in our affections. Hope has been ours. We have lived and laughed and sung and progressed.... But we have also wept and grieved.

Twice the doctor had said we were to conquer. Then came last spring and the end of hope. Week after week, Marjorie saw the sunbeams filter through the windows of her open porch; near by, a pair of robins built their nest; she watched them and knew them and named them. We planned great things together and great journeys we should make. That they were not to be she never knew.... And then she fell asleep....

Her little life had fulfilled its mission. She had brought joy and beauty and faith into our hearts; she had comforted us in our hours of loneliness and despair; she had been the little cheerful builder of our home--and perhaps God needed her.

She continued to sleep for three days, only for those three days her sun porch was a bower of roses. On Memorial Day, Mother and I stood once more together beside a little mound where God had led us. Late that afternoon we returned to the home to which Marjorie had taken us. It had grown more lovely with the beauty which has been ours, because of her.

*   *   *   *   *

The home is not yet completed. We still cherish our dreams of what it is to be. We would change this and that. But, after all, what the home is to be is not within our power to say. We hope to go forward together, building and changing and improving it. To-morrow shall see something that was not there yesterday. But through sun and shade, through trial and through days of ease and of peace, it is our hope that something of our best shall still remain. Whatever happens, it is our hope that what may be "just a house" to many shall be to us the home we have been building for the last fifteen years.

HOME
By Edgar A. Guest

It takes a heap o' livin' in a house t' make it home,
A heap o' sun an' shadder, an' ye sometimes have t' roam
Afore ye really 'preciate the things ye lef' behind,
An' hunger fer 'em somehow, with 'em allus on yer mind.
It don't make any differunce how rich ye get t' be,
How much yer chairs an' tables cost, how great yer luxury;
It ain't home t' ye, though it be the palace of a king,
Until somehow yer soul is sort o' wrapped round everything.

Home ain't a place that gold can buy or get up in a minute;
Afore it's home there's got t' be a heap o' livin' in it;
Within the walls there's got t' be some babies born, and then
Right there ye've got t' bring 'em up t' women good, an' men;
And gradjerly, as time goes on, ye find ye wouldn't part
With anything they ever used--they've grown into yer heart:
The old high chairs, the playthings, too, the little shoes they wore

Ye hoard; an' if ye could ye'd keep the thumbmarks on the door.
Ye've got t' weep t' make it home, ye've got t' sit an' sigh

An' watch beside a loved one's bed, an' know that Death is nigh;
An' in the stillness o' the night t' see Death's angel come,
An' close the eyes o' her that smiled, an' leave her sweet voice dumb.
Fer these are scenes that grip the heart, an' when yer tears are dried,
Ye find the home is dearer than it was, an' sanctified;
An' tuggin' at ye always are the pleasant memories
O' her that was an' is no more--ye can't escape from these.

Ye've got t' sing an' dance fer years, ye've got t' romp an' play,
An' learn t' love the things ye have by usin' 'em each day;
Even the roses 'round the porch must blossom year by year
Afore they 'come a part o' ye, suggestin' someone dear
Who used t' love 'em long ago, an' trained 'em jes' t' run
The way they do, so's they would get the early mornin' sun;
Ye've got t' love each brick an' stone from cellar up t' dome:
It takes a heap o' livin' in a house t' make it home.

[From "A Heap o' Livin'"]

The Codes Of Hammurabi And Moses
W. W. Davies

QTY

The discovery of the Hammurabi Code is one of the greatest achievements of archaeology, and is of paramount interest, not only to the student of the Bible, but also to all those interested in ancient history...

Religion   **ISBN:** *1-59462-338-4*   **Pages:132**
MSRP $12.95

The Theory of Moral Sentiments
Adam Smith

QTY

This work from 1749. contains original theories of conscience amd moral judgment and it is the foundation for systemof morals.

Philosophy **ISBN:** *1-59462-777-0*   **Pages:536**
MSRP $19.95

Jessica's First Prayer
Hesba Stretton

QTY

In a screened and secluded corner of one of the many railway-bridges which span the streets of London there could be seen a few years ago, from five o'clock every morning until half past eight, a tidily set-out coffee-stall, consisting of a trestle and board, upon which stood two large tin cans, with a small fire of charcoal burning under each so as to keep the coffee boiling during the early hours of the morning when the work-people were thronging into the city on their way to their daily toil...

Childrens   **ISBN:** *1-59462-373-2*   **Pages:84**
MSRP $9.95

My Life and Work
Henry Ford

QTY

Henry Ford revolutionized the world with his implementation of mass production for the Model T automobile. Gain valuable business insight into his life and work with his own auto-biography... "We have only started on our development of our country we have not as yet, with all our talk of wonderful progress, done more than scratch the surface. The progress has been wonderful enough but..."

Biographies/   **ISBN:** *1-59462-198-5*   **Pages:300**
MSRP $21.95

www.bookjungle.com *email: sales@bookjungle.com fax: 630-214-0564 mail: Book Jungle PO Box 2226 Champaign, IL 61825*

The Art of Cross-Examination
Francis Wellman

QTY

I presume it is the experience of every author, after his first book is published upon an important subject, to be almost overwhelmed with a wealth of ideas and illustrations which could readily have been included in his book, and which to his own mind, at least, seem to make a second edition inevitable. Such certainly was the case with me; and when the first edition had reached its sixth impression in five months, I rejoiced to learn that it seemed to my publishers that the book had met with a sufficiently favorable reception to justify a second and considerably enlarged edition. ...

Pages:412

Reference   **ISBN:** *1-59462-647-2*   *MSRP $19.95*

On the Duty of Civil Disobedience
Henry David Thoreau

QTY

Thoreau wrote his famous essay, On the Duty of Civil Disobedience, as a protest against an unjust but popular war and the immoral but popular institution of slave-owning. He did more than write—he declined to pay his taxes, and was hauled off to gaol in consequence. Who can say how much this refusal of his hastened the end of the war and of slavery ?

Law   **ISBN:** *1-59462-747-9*   **Pages:48**

MSRP $7.45

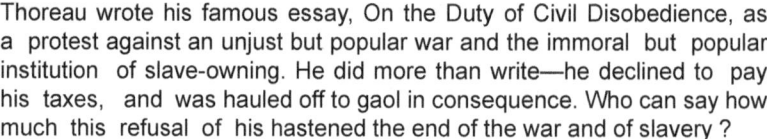

Dream Psychology Psychoanalysis for Beginners
Sigmund Freud

QTY

Sigmund Freud, born Sigismund Schlomo Freud (May 6, 1856 - September 23, 1939), was a Jewish-Austrian neurologist and psychiatrist who co-founded the psychoanalytic school of psychology. Freud is best known for his theories of the unconscious mind, especially involving the mechanism of repression; his redefinition of sexual desire as mobile and directed towards a wide variety of objects; and his therapeutic techniques, especially his understanding of transference in the therapeutic relationship and the presumed value of dreams as sources of insight into unconscious desires.

Pages:196

Psychology   **ISBN:** *1-59462-905-6*   *MSRP $15.45*

The Miracle of Right Thought
Orison Swett Marden

QTY

Believe with all of your heart that you will do what you were made to do. When the mind has once formed the habit of holding cheerful, happy, prosperous pictures, it will not be easy to form the opposite habit. It does not matter how improbable or how far away this realization may see, or how dark the prospects may be, if we visualize them as best we can, as vividly as possible, hold tenaciously to them and vigorously struggle to attain them, they will gradually become actualized, realized in the life. But a desire, a longing without endeavor, a yearning abandoned or held indifferently will vanish without realization.

Pages:360

Self Help   **ISBN:** *1-59462-644-8*   *MSRP $25.45*

The Rosicrucian Cosmo-Conception Mystic Christianity *by Max Heindel*   ISBN: *1-59462-188-8*   **$38.95**

The Rosicrucian Cosmo-conception is not dogmatic, neither does it appeal to any other authority than the reason of the student. It is: not controversial, but is: sent forth in the, hope that it may help to clear...   New Age/Religion Pages 646

Abandonment To Divine Providence *by Jean-Pierre de Caussade*   ISBN: *1-59462-228-0*   **$25.95**

"The Rev. Jean Pierre de Caussade was one of the most remarkable spiritual writers of the Society of Jesus in France in the 18th Century. His death took place at Toulouse in 1751. His works have gone through many editions and have been republished...   Inspirational/Religion Pages 400

Mental Chemistry *by Charles Haanel*   ISBN: *1-59462-192-6*   **$23.95**

Mental Chemistry allows the change of material conditions by combining and appropriately utilizing the power of the mind. Much like applied chemistry creates something new and unique out of careful combinations of chemicals the mastery of mental chemistry...   New Age Pages 354

The Letters of Robert Browning and Elizabeth Barret Barrett 1845-1846 vol II   ISBN: *1-59462-193-4*   **$35.95**

by Robert Browning and Elizabeth Barrett   Biographies Pages 596

Gleanings In Genesis (volume I) *by Arthur W. Pink*   ISBN: *1-59462-130-6*   **$27.45**

Appropriately has Genesis been termed "the seed plot of the Bible" for in it we have, in germ form, almost all of the great doctrines which are afterwards fully developed in the books of Scripture which follow...   Religion/Inspirational Pages 420

The Master Key *by L. W. de Laurence*   ISBN: *1-59462-001-6*   **$30.95**

In no branch of human knowledge has there been a more lively increase of the spirit of research during the past few years than in the study of Psychology, Concentration and Mental Discipline. The requests for authentic lessons in Thought Control, Mental Discipline and...   New Age/Business Pages 422

The Lesser Key Of Solomon Goetia *by L. W. de Laurence*   ISBN: *1-59462-092-X*   **$9.95**

This translation of the first book of the "Lemegton" which is now for the first time made accessible to students of Talismanic Magic was done, after careful collation and edition, from numerous Ancient Manuscripts in Hebrew, Latin, and French...   New Age/Occult Pages 92

Rubaiyat Of Omar Khayyam *by Edward Fitzgerald*   ISBN: *1-59462-332-5*   **$13.95**

Edward Fitzgerald, whom the world has already learned, in spite of his own efforts to remain within the shadow of anonymity, is to look upon as one of the rarest poets of the century, was born at Bredfield, in Suffolk, on the 31st of March, 1809. He was the third son of John Purcell...   Music Pages 172

Ancient Law *by Henry Maine*   ISBN: *1-59462-128-4*   **$29.95**

The chief object of the following pages is to indicate some of the earliest ideas of mankind, as they are reflected in Ancient Law, and to point out the relation of those ideas to modern thought.   Religiom/History Pages 452

Far-Away Stories *by William J. Locke*   ISBN: *1-59462-129-2*   **$19.45**

"Good wine needs no bush, but a collection of mixed vintages does. And this book is just such a collection. Some of the stories I do not want to remain buried for ever in the museum files of dead magazine-numbers an author's not unpardonable vanity..."   Fiction Pages 272

Life of David Crockett *by David Crockett*   ISBN: *1-59462-250-7*   **$27.45**

"Colonel David Crockett was one of the most remarkable men of the times in which he lived. Born in humble life, but gifted with a strong will, an indomitable courage, and unremitting perseverance...   Biographies/New Age Pages 424

Lip-Reading *by Edward Nitchie*   ISBN: *1-59462-206-X*   **$25.95**

Edward B. Nitchie, founder of the New York School for the Hard of Hearing, now the Nitchie School of Lip-Reading, Inc, wrote "LIP-READING Principles and Practice". The development and perfecting of this meritorious work on lip-reading was an undertaking...   How-to Pages 400

A Handbook of Suggestive Therapeutics, Applied Hypnotism, Psychic Science   ISBN: *1-59462-214-0*   **$24.95**

by Henry Munro   Health/New Age/Health/Self-help Pages 376

A Doll's House: and Two Other Plays *by Henrik Ibsen*   ISBN: *1-59462-112-8*   **$19.95**

Henrik Ibsen created this classic when in revolutionary 1848 Rome. Introducing some striking concepts in playwriting for the realist genre, this play has been studied the world over.   Fiction/Classics/Plays 308

The Light of Asia *by sir Edwin Arnold*   ISBN: *1-59462-204-3*   **$13.95**

In this poetic masterpiece, Edwin Arnold describes the life and teachings of Buddha. The man who was to become known as Buddha to the world was born as Prince Gautama of India but he rejected the worldly riches and abandoned the reigns of power when...   Religion/History/Biographies Pages 170

The Complete Works of Guy de Maupassant *by Guy de Maupassant*   ISBN: *1-59462-157-8*   **$16.95**

"For days and days, nights and nights, I had dreamed of that first kiss which was to consecrate our engagement, and I knew not on what spot I should put my lips..."   Fiction/Classics Pages 240

The Art of Cross-Examination *by Francis L. Wellman*   ISBN: *1-59462-309-0*   **$26.95**

Written by a renowned trial lawyer, Wellman imparts his experience and uses case studies to explain how to use psychology to extract desired information through questioning.   How-to/Science/Reference Pages 408

Answered or Unanswered? *by Louisa Vaughan*   ISBN: *1-59462-248-5*   **$10.95**

Miracles of Faith in China   Religion Pages 112

The Edinburgh Lectures on Mental Science (1909) *by Thomas*   ISBN: *1-59462-008-3*   **$11.95**

This book contains the substance of a course of lectures recently given by the writer in the Queen Street Hail, Edinburgh. Its purpose is to indicate the Natural Principles governing the relation between Mental Action and Material Conditions...   New Age/Psychology Pages 148

Ayesha *by H. Rider Haggard*   ISBN: *1-59462-301-5*   **$24.95**

Verily and indeed it is the unexpected that happens! Probably if there was one person upon the earth from whom the Editor of this, and of a certain previous history, did not expect to hear again...   Classics Pages 380

Ayala's Angel *by Anthony Trollope*   ISBN: *1-59462-352-X*   **$29.95**

The two girls were both pretty, but Lucy who was twenty-one who supposed to be simple and comparatively unattractive, whereas Ayala was credited, as her Bombwhat romantic name might show, with poetic charm and a taste for romance. Ayala when her father died was nineteen...   Fiction Pages 484

The American Commonwealth *by James Bryce*   ISBN: *1-59462-286-8*   **$34.45**

An interpretation of American democratic political theory. It examines political mechanics and society from the perspective of Scotsman James Bryce   Politics Pages 572

Stories of the Pilgrims *by Margaret P. Pumphrey*   ISBN: *1-59462-116-0*   **$17.95**

This book explores pilgrims religious oppression in England as well as their escape to Holland and eventual crossing to America on the Mayflower, and their early days in New England...   History Pages 268

www.bookjungle.com *email: sales@bookjungle.com fax: 630-214-0564 mail: Book Jungle PO Box 2226 Champaign, IL 61825*

QTY

The Fasting Cure *by Sinclair Upton*   ISBN: *1-59462-222-1*   **$13.95**
*In the Cosmopolitan Magazine for May, 1910, and in the Contemporary Review (London) for April, 1910, I published an article dealing with my experi-
ences in fasting. I have written a great many magazine articles, but never one which attracted so much attention... New Age/Self Help/Health Pages 164*

Hebrew Astrology *by Sepharial*   ISBN: *1-59462-308-2*   **$13.45**
*In these days of advanced thinking it is a matter of common observation that we have left many of the old landmarks behind and that we are now pressing
forward to greater heights and to a wider horizon than that which represented the mind-content of our progenitors...   Astrology Pages 144*

Thought Vibration or The Law of Attraction in the Thought World   ISBN: *1-59462-127-6*   **$12.95**

by William Walker Atkinson   *Psychology/Religion Pages 144*

Optimism *by Helen Keller*   ISBN: *1-59462-108-X*   **$15.95**
*Helen Keller was blind, deaf, and mute since 19 months old, yet famously learned how to overcome these handicaps, communicate with the world, and
spread her lectures promoting optimism. An inspiring read for everyone...   Biographies/Inspirational Pages 84*

Sara Crewe *by Frances Burnett*   ISBN: *1-59462-360-0*   **$9.45**
*In the first place, Miss Minchin lived in London. Her home was a large, dull, tall one, in a large, dull square, where all the houses were alike, and all the
sparrows were alike, and where all the door-knockers made the same heavy sound...   Childrens/Classic Pages 88*

The Autobiography of Benjamin Franklin *by Benjamin Franklin*   ISBN: *1-59462-135-7*   **$24.95**
*The Autobiography of Benjamin Franklin has probably been more extensively read than any other American historical work, and no other book of its kind
has had such ups and downs of fortune. Franklin lived for many years in England, where he was agent...   Biographies/History Pages 332*

Name	
Email	
Telephone	
Address	
City, State ZIP	

☐ **Credit Card**   ☐ **Check / Money Order**

Credit Card Number	
Expiration Date	
Signature	

Please Mail to: Book Jungle
PO Box 2226
Champaign, IL 61825
or Fax to: 630-214-0564

ORDERING INFORMATION

web*: www.bookjungle.com*
email*: sales@bookjungle.com*
fax*: 630-214-0564*
mail*: Book Jungle PO Box 2226 Champaign, IL 61825*
or PayPal *to sales@bookjungle.com*

Please contact us for bulk discounts

DIRECT-ORDER TERMS

**20% Discount if You Order
Two or More Books**
Free Domestic Shipping!
Accepted: Master Card, Visa,
Discover, American Express